A Touch of FEAR

5 Light Horror Stories for the Faint of Heart

REBECCA M. SENESE

OTHER BOOKS BY REBECCA M. SENESE

The Night Killers

The Color of Blood: The Chronicles of Richard Damon

Wreck the Halls: 5 Christmas Horror Stories

Oh the Horror! 5 Horror Stories

By Howl & Claw: 5 Werewolf Stories

With a Bite: 5 Vampire Tales

Bad Ends: 5 Horror Stories

The Horror Within: 5 Horror Stories

The Beginners Guide to the Recently Deceased

Daily Bread

The In-Between Series
Book 1: A Reluctance of Blood
Book 2: A Remembrance of Flesh
Book 3: A Retribution of Soul

A Touch of FEAR

5 LIGHT HORROR STORIES FOR THE FAINT OF HEART

REBECCA M. SENESE

RFAR Publishing
Toronto, Canada

Published 2014 by RFAR Publishing
Toronto, Canada
http://www.RFARPublishing.com

This is a work of fiction. All characters appearing in this work are fictitious. Any resemblance to real persons, living or dear is purely coincidental.

Trade paper edition designed by Rebecca M. Senese
in InDesign CS5.5

Electronic editions designed by Rebecca M. Senese

Cover design: Rebecca M. Senese
Cover Image © StockedPhotos.com
Interior Images © huhulin / CanStockPhoto.com
Lisann / CanStockPhoto.com

ISBN: 978-1-927603-27-7

Publications Acknowledgement

"Wolf's Bane." First published in *Allegory*, 2010.

A Touch of FEAR

5 Light Horror Stories for the Faint of Heart

Table of Contents

Introduction

Welcome to *A Touch of Fear*, a compilation of some of my lighter horror stories. One of the things I enjoy about horror is the gradations within the genre. Some of it is quite intense, with extreme violence or visual descriptions of things that will haunt your dreams forever. But on the other side of the spectrum, we have the subtle horror, that sneaks up on us or maybe isn't even as horrific as we think.

Maybe it's just another way of living.

So if you like your horror a little on the lighter side, with maybe a bit of humour sprinkled in, or a bit of subtly that makes you shiver without being too scared, then this is the compilation for you.

Just a little bit of boo.

Just a little scream.

Enjoy!

Rebecca M. Senese
December 2013

How to Cook Husbands

Marjorie didn't notice the typo until she got the first batch of cookbooks back from the printers. "How to Cook Husbands" adorned the cover in bright red script, just above the photograph of a lovely cooked ham dinner. For a brief moment, Marjorie read it the correct way "How to Cook for Husbands." Then she read it aloud and realized the error.

"Oh dammit," she said.

Her sister, Ellen, wandered in from the kitchen, wiping her hands on a dish towel.

"What's wrong?"

"They got the title wrong. Look at this." Marjorie handed her a copy of the cookbook.

After a moment, Ellen burst out laughing.

"It's not funny," Marjorie said.

"It sure is! I know several women who'd love to know how to cook their husbands." She wiped her eyes with the towel.

"This is a fund raiser for the community centre," Marjorie said. "They paid for the printing and it's all ruined."

Ellen's laughter trickled away. "Oh. Um, maybe we can sell them as a gag."

"I don't think they'd go for that." She dropped the book back into the carton. "Almost ten grand, gone. They took a chance on it. I had to talk them into it and now it's ruined."

"Listen, it's not that bad." Ellen picked up the book again and thumbed through it. "The recipes are great. I think you should still sell it."

"Don't be ridiculous. The community centre would never go for it."

"Okay, how about this? We sell it online. We don't have to have any affiliation with the community centre but you hand over the money to them. That way they still get the funds but don't have to be associated with it."

Marjorie chewed on her lower lip, a habit she learned from their mother. "I don't know."

"Come on," Ellen said. "It could work. I bet ladies would love it. It's good for a laugh and your recipes are wonderful." She nudged her sister.

Marjorie sighed. "I don't know anything about selling online."

"Don't worry about that," Ellen said. "Leave it to me. Suzanne down the street's got an online store. She can help."

Before Marjorie could protest, Ellen dropped the towel on the dining table and headed out the front door, carrying a copy of the mis-titled cookbook with her.

By the end of the week Ellen had worked her magic and the new website for "How to Cook Husbands" was live and waiting for the first orders. Sitting beside Ellen in front of the laptop on the dining room table, Marjorie shook her head.

"I don't believe this will work," she said.

"Why not?" Ellen said. "It's a great gimmick. Your turkey surprise is worth the price of the book. It's all about getting attention. Next thing we have to do is create a little video for it."

"A video? What about?"

"Talk about the book and the recipes. Wink at the camera, like a joke that the ingredients aren't really supposed to be their husbands."

Marjorie sighed. "This is stupid."

"Sure it is but it might get some orders. Come on, Marj, let's give it a shot!"

Why she let her sister talk her into it, Marjorie didn't know, but it had always been that way. No matter what the wild scheme, Ellen wanted to go for it and always dragged Marjorie along for the ride. No matter how much she wanted to, she could never say no to Ellen. It had been that way for over fifty years, Ellen proposing an idea and Marjorie protesting but going along anyway. What else could she do? She had always doted on her younger sister.

Ellen borrowed a video camera from Suzanne down the street and they set it up in the kitchen.

Marjorie wore her favourite apron, black with blue flowers on it. She held up the cookbook and displayed her prized recipe for turkey surprise, emphasizing the importance of fresh herbs and spices. At Ellen's urging, she made a special note *not* to use husbands in this recipe and even winked at the camera.

"Not bad," Ellen said. "Turn your head a bit to the right this time. I'm getting a shadow across your face."

Five takes later, they had it or so Ellen said. She headed for the office and the laptop to edit and upload the footage. Marjorie decided she might as well make use of the ingredients they had out and actually make her turkey surprise. It was more than enough for the two of them for dinner. She called Suzanne and another few friends to see if they wanted to come by for dinner.

Several hours later, four of them sat around the dining table, the remains of the meal scattered across the table top. Barbara, one of Marjorie's friends, raised her wine glass.

"To another delicious meal," she said.

"Here here," Suzanne seconded.

They all raised their glasses and drank. Marjorie smiled at them.

"Thanks for coming by. I didn't want to make the turkey surprise and let it go to waste."

"This is my favourite recipe of yours," Barbara said. "This and the caramel butter custard."

"That sounds great," Suzanne said. "Very decadent."

"Speaking of decadent," Ellen piped up. "Let's see how your video is doing."

"Video?" Barbara said.

Marjorie sighed. "It's the whole cookbook thing. Ellen decided we needed to do a video to help promote it."

"That's a great idea," Suzanne said.

Marjorie shook her head. "Oh it's silly. The whole thing is preposterous. Who's going to buy a cookbook about cooking their husbands?"

Ellen returned, carrying the laptop cradled in her hands. "Looks like a few people are interested in it."

She pushed her plate aside and set the laptop on the table. Carrying their wine glasses, the women gathered around as Ellen sat down. She pulled up the video about the turkey surprise recipe from How To Cook Husbands. Marjorie sucked in a breath at the site of the graph with the line sloping straight up.

"What is that?"

"That is the number of views," Ellen said. "I posted this just before dinner a few hours ago, it's already past two thousand." She refreshed the screen and the number leaped again.

"That's crazy," Marjorie said.

Suzanne patted her shoulder. "Looks like you're popular, Marj. You should make another video."

Ellen's eyes lit up. "Definitely! One of the dessert recipes. And make more references to husbands."

Marjorie backed away, shaking her head. "No, that's enough. One video is enough. It's just a fluke. No one has anything better to do on a Sunday night. We haven't even sold any cookbooks."

"Well, let me just check the email." Ellen tapped at the keyboard. The screen changed. Ellen squealed.

"Ten orders already!"

"You have to do another video, Marj," Suzanne said. "You're a hit!"

"Ten isn't that much," Marjorie said. "It costs more than that to buy the ingredients."

"If you make the caramel butter custard, I'll buy the ingredients as long as I get to take it home." Barbara piped up.

"Come on, Marj," Ellen said. The familiar eager grin spread across her face, daring Marjorie forward. As always, Marjorie felt her resolve weaken in front of her sister's enthusiasm.

"Well, I do like making that custard," she said.

Before she spoke another word, the ladies were in motion, clearing the table and pulling out the camera.

"I don't have all the ingredients," Marjorie said.

Barbara grabbed a copy of the book. "I'll pick them up! Be back in half an hour." She ducked out the front door.

"Wear that same apron," Suzanne said. "But a different top underneath. Something light, maybe yellow. And no print. It's too busy on the camera."

By the time she was satisfied with Marjorie's attire, Barbara had returned with the ingredients.

She and Ellen arranged them on the counter in kitchen.

"Now do the same thing," Ellen said. "Remember to mention not really using husbands."

"Drink this first," Suzanne said. "Loosen up a bit." She poured Marjorie a glass of wine.

A few more hours and they had a new video ready for posting and dessert for enjoying. As Marjorie served the caramel butter custard, Ellen reviewed the video and prepared it for posting.

"Don't you have to do more editing?" Marjorie said.

"No, you were smoother on this one," Ellen said.

"Maybe it was those three glasses of wine," Suzanne said.

Marjorie pursed her lips as the ladies laughed. She tried to hold her own laughter in but lost out. Soon she laughed along with them.

"Shut up and eat your dessert!"

The next morning, Ellen came running into the kitchen as Marjorie poured the coffee. Ellen almost slammed the laptop down on the counter, making Marjorie jump a little. The coffee pot jiggled in her hand and she barely avoided spilling.

"Watch it, Ellen! What's the matter with you?"

"Marjorie, we've got orders for over two hundred cookbooks."

Marjorie poured milk into her coffee and stirred. "Don't be ridiculous."

"Take a look." Ellen turned the laptop toward her. The list scrolled down the screen and kept going as Ellen hit the page down button. Again and again. And again.

Marjorie stopped stirring, staring at the screen.

"Those are cookbook orders?"

"They sure are." Ellen grabbed her arm and squeezed. "Marj, you're a hit!"

Marjorie felt like she sleptwalked through the day until she got home in the evening. Ellen was already in the living room, surrounded by padded envelopes.

"Good, you're home. Start stuffing." Ellen pointed at a stack of envelopes by the overstuffed green armchair.

"We have to get these packages up as soon as possible."

"What's the rush?" Marjorie said. She stuck a cookbook in an envelope and included a folded invoice at Ellen's direction.

"Oh no rush," Ellen said. "We only got another two hundred orders this afternoon."

She laughed as Marjorie dropped the envelope, spilling the book out on the floor.

"Be careful with that," Ellen said. "We want our customers to be happy with their copies."

Marjorie picked up the book and shoved it into the envelope. "I can't believe so many people are buying the book."

"It's you," Ellen said. "You're a hit! Almost every order mentions your recipe videos and the numbers have jumped through the roof. We have to do another one."

"Oh no." Marjorie shook her head and found her hands were shaking as well. "I can't do another one."

"But you've got to, Marj! People love them and they're buying the cookbook. Just think of all the money you're earning for the community centre."

Ellen used her favourite pleading expression, the one Marjorie had never been able to resist since they were kids. Even now it made Marjorie uncomfortable to see the mix of eagerness and distress on her sister's face.

"Well, maybe one more."

That evening they created three more videos, each on a different type of meal; breakfast, lunch, and a quick dinner using regular, what's ever in the fridge sort of food. By eleven o'clock, Marjorie slumped over the kitchen table as Ellen turned off the camera.

"No more," she said.

"That's fine. We've got enough for a week or so," Ellen said. She carried the camera out of the room, missing Marjorie's hmph of exasperation.

Left with several meals, Marjorie packaged it up and stuffed it into fridge. She'd be having leftovers at the office this week. At least there was a selection.

The next day, orders for the cookbook doubled and then doubled again two days later. By the end of the week Ellen suggested a stuffing party to help keep up with the packaging. Supplying cheese, crackers and wine, Marjorie, Ellen, Suzanne and Barbara sat around the living room, stuffing cookbooks into envelopes.

By ten, Marjorie's fingers ached. She took a break to pour herself another glass of wine. Unfortunately the white held none of its chill from earlier in the evening but it was still better than nothing, she thought as she sipped.

"I'll be glad when this is over," she said. "I'm getting tired of stuffing envelopes."

"For the next print run, we'll do it POD. Let someone else deal with the headaches of packing and shipping," Ellen said.

"What do you mean next print run?"

Ellen folded over an envelope flap and tossed it onto the growing pile of finished orders. "When we finish this print run and we reorder."

"No, I'm done."

"How can you say that? You've got a hit on your hands."

"It's a silly gimmick, that's all. I don't want to be stuck with tons of copies."

"That's the beauty of POD," Ellen said. "You aren't stuck with copies. We'll push to sell these and then let it go on its own. It'll practically run itself."

"Then you can write the next one," Suzanne said.

Marjorie frowned. "You aren't helping."

"Come on, Marj, don't tell me you don't have any more recipes."

"Maybe you can even include one using an actual husband," Barbara quipped.

The ladies laughed. Marjorie hid her unease by sipping her wine. It was supposed to be a joke but there was something malicious behind her friends' laughter. She didn't think she wanted to know what it was.

After Suzanne and Barbara left and Ellen retired to her room, Marjorie sat at the dining table with the laptop open to "her" video channel. Even as she watched, the number of views rose. Sipping her wine, she scrolled through the comments. Most discussed the recipes, liking the easiness of them and the humour of 'cooking husbands.' But some of the comments seem to take it a little too seriously.

But that's the Internet, isn't it, Marjorie thought. People could be anonymous and say anything that came into their head without thinking. They didn't really mean it, not when they stopped to think of it.

She had to believe that.

Finally at half past one, she logged off and went to bed. She dreamed of a gigantic roasting pan. She was having to lift a huge shovel in order to do the basting. As she hoisted it on her shoulders and tottered toward the pan, she peered over the edge to look at the giant turkey. But it wasn't a turkey. It was Suzanne's husband, Ray, lying facedown, arms trussed behind him, a succulent apple stuck in his mouth.

The scream stalled in her throat as she struggled to wake up. Weak sunlight peeked around her blinds. She stumbled out of bed and into the bathroom. Splashing cold water on her face chased the rest of the nightmare away.

Enough. That was enough. No more cookbooks.

She avoided Ellen that morning by heading off to the market early. A few hours poking around the various stalls would do her good. She started at the craft area and worked her way over to the food section, selecting food for the week's groceries. Just before noon, she finished and headed home, feeling refreshed and rejuvenated.

She had decided that it really was enough. She'd finish selling this batch for the community centre and that was it. If Ellen wanted to continue, she could do without Marjorie, pouting or not.

This time, Marjorie would maintain her resolve.

When she turned onto the street, she noticed a police car parked across from the house. Strange. Had the Templeton boy been caught shoplifting again? Marjorie pulled the car into the driveway and retrieved the bags from the truck. As she headed up the front walk, trying to juggle the bags in her arms and reach for her keys, the door opened. Ellen stood in the doorway. She grabbed one of the bags.

"Thanks," Marjorie said. "I got enough for a small army."

"We've got company." Ellen's somber expression stopped her.

"Who?"

Ellen leaned forward to grab a second bag. Her lips aimed for Marjorie's ear.

"The police," she whispered.

Marjorie sucked in a breath as she entered the house. Two police officers stood in front of the couch. Coffee cups set on the coffee table attested to how long they'd been there. Waiting for her?

"I'll take these into the kitchen," Ellen said. She hurried off, leaving Marjorie still holding one bag.

The officer in uniform stepped forward. "I can take that into the kitchen if you like."

"Sure." Marjorie handed it over.

The officer held the bag from the bottom and disappeared down the hall.

"I'm Detective Morgan," said the man in the brown suit. "We've been waiting for you to get home."

"I see," Marjorie said. "Won't you sit down?"

He returned to the couch as Marjorie sat in the overstuffed green armchair. Usually she loved this chair but now she felt like a child playing pretend in her mother's house.

"We just have a few questions," Detective Morgan said.

"Is there a problem?" Marjorie held her hands firmly in her lap. The urge to fidget was almost overwhelming.

Morgan tugged on his ear, reminding her of Carol Burnett on her old variety show. Hadn't

Carol tugged on her ear at the end of each show for some reason?

"We were called to a crime scene yesterday and your cookbook was found there," the detective said.

"My cookbook?"

"Yes. It was, um, rather strange circumstances." He tugged at his ear again. Why had Carol Burnett pulled on her ear? For some reason, it seemed vital that Marjorie remember this piece of trivia at this moment.

"I've never been involved in any crime," Marjorie said. "Well, I did once see the Templeton boy... but that's not anything really."

"I didn't think you were involved," the detective said. "But your cookbook did seem... well..."

"Did seem what?"

"To be of some inspiration," he finished.

Marjorie's hands flew apart and gripped the armrests. "What do you mean 'inspiration'?"

The detective tugged on his ear again. Definitely a nervous habit and one that made her want to slap his hand away. Why the hell had Burnett tugged on her ear that way?

"It appeared that the lady of the house used your cookbook in her preparations for the evening meal on Thursday," the detective said. "It involved her husband."

Saying hello to her grandmother. The answer popped into Marjorie's head. Carol Burnett had always tugged on her ear to say hello to her grandmother and to let her know Carol was okay. Marjorie wished she had someone like that looking out for her right now but she didn't feel like tugging on her ear. More like hiding under the bed.

"Involved her husband," she said.

The detective nodded. Marjorie waited but he didn't tug on his ear again. His hand now rested in his lap. He wasn't just going to tell her, she realized. She would have to ask.

She didn't want to.

"What did she do?"

Now the detective squirmed a little on the couch. "Well, there was a recipe that the book was opened up to," he said. "Something about a turkey surprise."

"Excuse me!"

Marjorie ran from the room and raced up the stairs.

"Marjorie!" Ellen's voice floated up the stairs after her but she slammed the bathroom door, cutting off the sound of her sister's voice. Marjorie leaned against the door. Her heart pounded in her chest. Her stomach twisted, as if trying to ring out any remnants of her own turkey surprise from last weekend. Images flashed in her head: deboning the legs, slicing open the main cavity, stuffing it with vegetables.

She barely managed to lift the toilet lid before she vomited.

Banging sounded on the door. Marjorie flushed the toilet and rinsed her mouth before opening the door. Her hand trembled, rattling the door knob.

Ellen stood in the doorway, forehead crinkled in concern. "Marjorie, what the hell?"

"That detective, he said they found my cookbook at a crime scene."

Ellen's frown deepened. "And?"

"And some woman used my recipe to cook her husband!" Marjorie's voice hissed out between her lips. She clenched them tight, trying to stop her urge to throw up again.

"Oh for heaven's sake," Ellen said. "That's not your fault. Obviously the lady is nuts. She would have killed her husband some other way. Come on, let me handle this."

Her hand tightened on Marjorie's arm and pulled her out into the hall. Marjorie followed her sister unwillingly. Her steps dragged on the stairs as they walked down. Both police officers stood in the living room, faces turned up to watch them descend the stairs. Ellen reached the room first and entered, crossing her arms across her chest.

"I don't appreciate you upsetting my sister," she said. "We had nothing to do with any crime. We're selling a cookbook and that's it."

"Your book was found at the crime scene," the detective said.

"I'm sure there were other books there as well," Ellen said. "Are you interrogating all the authors?"

"Ma'm, the woman used the cookbook…"

"We didn't have anything to do with that."

"The title of your book…"

"Was a printing error," Ellen said. "We decided

to sell it as a joke. You can't prosecute us for that. Now you've upset my sister and I think you should go."

The detective didn't look very happy. His hand reached up to his ear again but he didn't argue with Ellen. No one ever argued with Ellen, they always did things her way, even if they were reluctant like this detective. He frowned at her as he left, leading the uniformed officer out onto the porch. Ellen closed the door in his face.

"Can you believe that?" Ellen said. "As if we had anything to do with that."

She shook her head. "Come on, let's get some tea. We got another huge batch of orders over night."

Marjorie followed her into the kitchen, watching as Ellen busied herself getting the tea ready. Kettle filled with water, tea pot filled with tea, cups and saucers pulled out of cupboards. She even pulled out a box of shortbread cookies.

"We need a treat after that nonsense," she said.

Marjorie didn't reply. She sat at the kitchen table, feeling the hard wooden back of the chair pressed against her spine. If she pushed herself hard enough against it, it would keep her upright, keep her from sagging within herself. A woman had killed her husband, using Marjorie's cookbook as inspiration. How could she live with that?

Ellen set the tea cup in front of her and sat across to pour. The fragrant steam teased Marjorie's nostrils but she didn't feel like drinking. Ellen set two cookies on a small plate and slid it in front of her.

"Your favourite," she said.

"I'm not hungry," Marjorie said.

"Don't be like that, Marj. It's not your fault. The lady was nuts. It wasn't your cookbook. If it was there'd be dozens like that and there aren't. I'm already getting emails from people saying how much they enjoy the recipes. Don't you see how much pleasure it's giving people? Don't let this one thing spoil it."

Ellen was right, Marjorie thought, Ellen was always right, even when she was wrong. Marjorie just didn't have the energy to fight her, never had. It had always been easier to give in, to go along, to follow behind her larger than life sister. She'd been content to stay in the shadows, to always be the last one noticed. It never bothered her. But this was her cookbook, her baby. She'd been the one to talk to the community centre about it, persuaded them to give her the opportunity for fund raising. Ellen had never been involved. It had been all Marjorie's, until that typo.

How to Cook Husbands.

"Drink your tea," Ellen said. "We'll tackle those orders after this snack. We're going through this print run in record time. I really think we should look into the POD option." She continued on, outlining her plans to expand the line, do more videos, push it for bigger sales.

Marjorie sipped her tea, listening to her sister's voice drone on and on, dulling to a low vibration in her skull. Ellen had taken over, the way she always had, the dolls and dream houses, the boys in high school, on and on. Every idea, every thought Marjorie ever had became co-opted and refined by Ellen, even the cookbook.

Her cookbook.

"We should think about writing a sequel," Ellen's voice drifted in her mind.

Yes, a sequel. Marjorie realized she was already thinking along the same lines and had been for several days now. Not surprising that after all of these years that she and Ellen were on the same track, heading in the same direction. Marjorie already had ideas about ingredients and spices, cooking times and butchery methods. Yes, a sequel was quite in order. And she even knew what she wanted to call it.

How to Cook Family.

Wolf's Bane

Mrs. Willis was a deep sleeper and didn't hear the phone until the fifth ring. Blinking, she sputtered awake, her voice a gravely beast in her throat as she croaked, "Fred, can you get that?"

The phone continued to ring. Must have gone to the shop early, Mrs. Willis thought fuzzily. She stumbled out of bed and groped into the hall.

"Hello?"

"Eva, is that you?"

Mrs. Willis sighed. "Of course, it's me, Joan. Who else would it be?"

"Oh yes, well, have you seen Fred today?"

Mrs. Willis rubbed sleep from her eyes. Being woken from a deep sleep didn't give her a good temperament for twenty questions.

"No, Joan, he's probably left for the shop."

"Oh, um, well, okay, it's probably nothing then."

Mrs. Willis closed her eyes and ran a hand through her greying hair. Take a deep breath, Eva, she told herself.

"What's nothing, Joan?"

"Oh well, Eva, I was just getting a snack last night. Felt a bit peckish and thought some soup would soothe my nerves..."

Mrs. Willis's fist tightened in her hair. Her jaw clenched. If Joan Davis stood in front of her right now she didn't know if she could resist the temptation to bite her square on her fat nose. Be calm, she reminded herself. Her mother had always told her that a bad temper wasn't lady-like.

"I usually like tomato but that's a little acidic, so I thought..."

"Joan!"

"Oh yes, um, right. So I was down in the kitchen and I heard a car driving by. Not very fast, rather slow actually. In fact, it stopped, outside the house. I saw it when I looked out the living room window."

"Well, that's a great story, Joan," Mrs. Willis said. "I really have to be going."

"No, wait, Eva. The truck, I saw writing on it. It said 'Dog Catcher.'"

Mrs. Willis dropped the phone.

She checked the entire house, including the sub-basement with the crawl space in front and the attic. Nothing, nada, zip. Standing in the hallway, dust bunnies from the basement tangled in her hair, Mrs. Willis clutched her flannel night-gown to her chest.

Oh god, a dog catcher.

Hadn't they moved from the city to avoid them, the pound, the Humane Society? Can't enter this park without a leash, poop'n scoop, every dog must have a license and shots. They'd specifically moved out of Toronto to avoid the traps. Now...

Fred, oh Fred.

Why didn't you wake me, she thought, staring at the heavy leather leash that hung on a nail outside the bedroom door. But she knew the answer to that one.

Fred didn't like to be a bother.

There was still time, it was still early. Just after seven. The sun was only now giving some consideration to rising, but it wouldn't make up its mind to start for at least half an hour.

Mrs. Willis hunched over the steering wheel of the old Honda. The traffic was unbelievable, even at this early hour. She had to refrain from blaring her horn at every idiot that got in the way. Getting a ticket for reckless driving wasn't going to help.

Why did the pound have to be so far from her house? She'd gotten the address from information. A new place, just opened a week ago. Wonderful. A new county ordinance. Well, she knew what she thought of their new ordinance. She imagined Fred would be quite graphic in his display.

The traffic crept along until she thought she was going to go mad. Finally her turnoff became visible in the distance. A fast check of her watch told her it was seven twenty. She tapped her wedding band on the steering wheel.

If her mother knew about this she'd be snickering right now, Mrs. Willis knew. She'd always disapproved of Fred, too wild, too impulsive for his own good. Of course, she didn't know the half of it. But after growing up the daughter of a reverend and with a mother determined to protect her from the stress and evils of the world, Mrs. Willis found she needed some wildness in her life. Fred's enthusiasm was just right and she'd supported him, even through the toughest times.

The turnoff, finally. She began to relax as she sped along the county road, leaving the clog of the highway behind. No radar traps here. She'd reach the pound with time to spare. Load Fred into the back seat and cover him up with the blanket for the ride home. The back windows were frosted so no one would be able to see in. Safe.

The pound was a tiny grey building set a ways back from the road. Mrs. Willis parked in the gravel parking lot in front. As she got out of the car, a chorus of barks drifted out from behind the building. That's where the pens are, she thought, clasping her purse to her breast. She listened for a moment, but couldn't discern Fred's voice.

The front door was locked but there was a buzzer next to it. Mrs. Willis leaned into it, listening to the echo behind the door. After a moment, a man's voice shouted.

"Alright, I'm coming!"

She released the buzzer and waited. Seconds crawled by until she began to root to the spot, the seasons changing around her as the days passed. Wind ruffled her hair, and she imagined it was the beginning of winter now although it was spring when she'd first set out. Then the door sprang open.

A hulking man peered down at her with bleary eyes. "Yeah?"

"I think you picked up my dog last night," Mrs. Willis said. "I've come to claim him."

The man blinked at her, then rubbed a hand over his bristly cheek. "Come in."

She followed him into the tiny waiting room and stood in front of the Formica counter while he crossed to the back. He opened a ledger and peered down at it. Mrs. Willis waited, resisting the impulse to tap her foot. She couldn't let the man see how impatient she was, how desperate.

"What kinda dog?" he asked.

"A mongrel really," she said. "Big, grey all over, long hair. Light blue eyes."

"Must have some husky in 'em," the man grunted. He turned a page casually in the ledger. Mrs. Willis restrained herself from digging her nails into his hand to make him move faster. Be calm, she thought. Her mother's warnings about the evils of stress flittered through her mind. She took deep breaths.

"Don't see anything in the ledger. Let me check the night receipts in the back office."

He turned away from her, shoving his hands in his pockets, not bothering to look up at her. Not only slow but rude as well, she thought. What was happening to courtesy these days? She peered over the counter top to look at the ledger. He'd conveniently closed it. How long would he be back in the office? Maybe she could take a quick peek.

The book was heavier than she thought and the pages flapped when she tried to pick it up.

A card fluttered out, landing on the counter. Quickly she snatched it up, about to stuff it back into the book.

"Richmond Breeders," the card read. Mrs. Willis clutched the card.

The dog catcher shuffled in from the back room. "Sorry, lady, didn't pick up any big mutts last night." He shrugged to emphasize the point.

He still wouldn't look at her. "Thank you for your help," Mrs. Willis said formally. She turned and walked precisely to her car.

Only when she'd started the engine and driven out of the parking lot and onto the county road again did she take the card from her pocket and read the address.

"Richmond Breeders," she murmured to herself. The address was almost an hour's drive. She swallowed, her fingertips whitening where she gripped the card.

She prayed she wouldn't be too late.

Fred Willis blinked at the bars of the pen. Even without a window he knew the sun was rising, he could feel it in his bones. They wanted to shift and stretch like a sleeping person upon awakening. But he was locked inside this pen and he couldn't allow himself to change now. Not when there would be witnesses. Not when *she* was here.

He stared over at the tall, dark brown bitch that curled up against the far wall of the pen. She noticed him looking at her and raised her sleek head. Quickly he looked away, scratching half heartedly at the dirt floor. He didn't want to have to fend her off again.

God, this was terrible, he thought, and embarrassing. If only he hadn't been so obsessed with that bloody squirrel he would have noticed the dog catcher and escaped. Now he was stuck here, in some breeder's pen, expected to do... To do.... He shuddered.

Of course, the worst thing was that the bitch tantalized him. Intellectually he knew it was merely pheromones; the bitch was in heat, but he couldn't deny that the idea had some allure and he felt ashamed. Imagine at his age, thinking such thoughts, it was disgraceful! And what about Eva?

They had a wonderful marriage and he never thought of cheating on her. But the breeder had already come back in twice, angry that nothing had happened yet. Fred had no idea what would happen if he came in a third time.

Could this even be defined as cheating? he wondered. He looked over at the bitch again. She was watching him, but didn't move, her head resting on her forepaws. She was just a dog, he knew, he could tell she wasn't like him. Could such a thing be considered adultery? It wasn't like he had many options.

Footsteps on the stairs raised the fur on his neck. Impulsively he growled low in his throat. He'd tried to cooperate with these people but it hadn't gotten him anywhere. Maybe it was time for some of the old fire.

Two men entered the basement wearing thick gloves and leather pants. The shorter one held a dart gun. The snarl died in Fred's throat. His heart pounded in his furry chest. Oh god, they meant to kill him, just because he hadn't...

"You sure about this?" the dark haired one asked. He gestured toward Fred.

The short man fiddled with the gun. "Guaranteed. This stuff would even get you started. Maybe I should sell some to your wife."

"Very funny. Just do it."

The gun aimed at Fred. Fred stood transfixed, staring at the barrel. He knew he should move, try to dodge, but while he was still considering it the gun spat. A needle pierced his shoulder and he yelped. Fire poured into his veins. With a snarl, Fred bit at the needle then lunged at the pen bars. The two men jumped back. The first one grinned.

"Seems pretty energetic now."

"Yeah, just you wait and see."

For Fred, the world began to tilt. He heard the men talking but it was white noise, nothing significant. He staggered away from the bars, trying to turn toward the back. He felt like he did when he had one too many beers at McMurphy's Pub.

The bitch rose and took at step toward him. Her musky smell enveloped him, strong and succulent. Fred blinked and tried to bark. It came out as a worble. Behind him, the men laughed.

Maybe it wasn't such a bad idea, he thought, looking at the bitch's sleek head, her muscular body. She wasn't a bad looking dog. Good teeth. Maybe just for a minute. Fred took a step.

The doorbell rang.

Mrs. Willis rang the bell again for good measure. She checked her watch for the tenth time, it was still eight forty-five.

Fred had to be here, she thought desperately. She didn't have any real proof, just the business card and her own instincts which had encouraged her the whole time she drove. She'd sped all the way, luckily avoiding any police. That too felt like confirmation. He was here, she could feel it.

Sort of.

Should she ring a third time? What if she was wrong and these people were asleep in their beds and she was rudely awakening them? She bit her lower lip. That guilt only added to her burden, making her shoulders hunch. This much stress was not good for her, not good for her constitution.

The door snatched open before her. Startled, Mrs. Willis gasped. A tall lanky man wearing leather pants and a tight dark shirt glared at her.

"Yeah?"

"Oh, I'm sorry to disturb you." Mrs. Willis struggled to regain her composure. "I understand you received a large grey dog from the Country dog catcher this morning."

If she'd guessed wrong, the man would simply deny it and then what? Nervously, she swallowed, twining her fingers in her purse strap.

"Sorry lady, we bought the mutt fair and square. Paid a good penny too. You'll have to take it up with the dog catcher."

Fred was here! "But you bought him illegally. I'm sure we could get the dog catcher to reimburse you."

"Forget it. It's your problem and he's my dog." He started to close the door.

Desperately, Mrs. Willis put her hand out to stop him.

"Wait, please, I'd be willing to pay."

The man rolled his eyes. "Go get another mutt, lady, I got plans for this one. Don't come here again or I'll charge you with trespassing." A nasty grin lit up the young man's thin face. "And don't bother going to the police either. All they'll find is doggy chops."

With a chuckle, he slammed the door in her face.

Mrs. Willis clutched her purse. Tears stung her eyes. Fred was here and no matter what vulgar things that young man said she wasn't going to let them keep Fred without a fight.

With a determined sniff, she set off to scout around the house.

"Who was that?"

The words sounded all strung together to Fred, a jumble of syllables. It helped to clear his head of the ringing he still heard.

"Some old bat looking for her dog," commented the man as he descended the stairs. He gestured loosely at the pen.

Fred, who had turned to advance on the bitch again, stopped short. The second man's words had sounded more distinct. *Old bat.* What did that mean? His mind felt fuzzy. Growling, he shook his head. He should remember, somehow he knew that. *Old bat.*

Eva!

A Touch of *FEAR*

The adrenaline rush the thought of her caused was too much for Fred. Too late he recognized the familiar tingling in his toes. Normally he could maintain his form for almost a full day if necessary, but this situation was anything but normal.

Fred let out a howl which shifted octaves to become a moan.

Dimly he was aware of the two men running toward the pen, shouting. But it was no longer important as his body began to transform. Fire raced through his body as his legs muscles shifted. Bones snapped under the internal pressure, grinding into a new configuration. His fur fell out in clumps, leaving his skin raw and itchy. Dimly he remembered how Eva had always stood at the ready with a full bottle of Vaseline intensive care lotion.

Snorting, he wiped fur from his eyes and stared through the bars at the two men. Both stood open mouthed, faces flushed with excitement and fear. In the far corner of the pen, the bitch cowered and whined. In a burst of movement, the younger man jumped back and scooped up his gun.

Fred staggered to his feet. His mouth tasted like gravel and fur. He coughed and tried to speak.

The younger man raised the gun. But a shadow moved on the stairs behind him and a beer case crashed down onto his head. The man dropped, the gun skidding across the floor.

Fred gripped the bars of the cage door and pushed. Metal groaned but didn't give. He had to try harder; soon he would be fully human with only the strength of an old man.

From the shadows on the stairway, Mrs. Willis stepped down. She dropped the beer case onto the body of the younger man. Across him, she faced the lanky man with leather pants.

"I told you he's mine," she snapped.

The lanky man lunged for the gun. Mrs Willis swung her purse to block him.

Fred's heart pounded in his chest. Vaguely he was aware of the bitch behind him, whining eagerly. With one final push, the bars snapped, spilling Fred onto the floor. The bitch leapt out after him.

He rolled and bounced to his feet, a foot away from where the man was aiming at Eva. At Eva! Rage flooded Fred, making his lips draw back from his teeth in a snarl.

His nails, still more claw than nail, sliced through the man's forearm, exposing slick muscle and bone. The man shrieked, numb fingers dropping the gun. He fell a moment later to his knees, clutching his ruined arm against him. The bitch jumped forward, snapping.

Fred turned to see Mrs Willis' white face. She gulped in air. He crossed to her and took her arm.

"It's all right, dear. You mustn't strain yourself."

She nodded and took several deep breaths. "I'm fine now, dear."

He patted her cheek and turned back to the groaning man.

"I don't know if you can hear me," he said. "But this is the consequences of your thoughtless actions. Your arm will heal, but you'll be changed from now on."

"Fred," Mrs Willis interrupted.

"Yes, dear?"

She fiddled with her belt, a sure sign that she had something unpleasant to say. "I don't think he should. I mean, he's not a very nice man."

Fred pursed his lips. He couldn't just kill the man, not like this. He would be no better than these hoodlums.

"What else can we do, Eva?"

A smile touched her wrinkled face, reminding him of her smile so long ago, on a smooth face full of trust and love.

"I think there's someone else here who deserves it more."

She reached out and patted the bitch's head. The bitch wagged her tail, trying to nuzzle the old woman's hand. Mrs Willis chuckled.

"She's so friendly," she said. "I hate the thought of giving her to that wretched dog catcher. He lied to me about finding you. Imagine what he would do to her." She scratched the dog's throat. The dog closed her eyes with pleasure.

"Besides," Mrs Willis continued. "You'll need someone to look after you when you hunt. Goodness knows you can't do it yourself."

Fred studied the dog. He'd never changed an animal before. "She'll need a lot of food for a few days," he said. "I don't think we have anything at home."

"Oh Fred, don't be silly," Mrs Willis said. "There's plenty here for her."

"Of course," Fred said. "Hold her still, will you, dear?"

Afterward, Mrs Willis helped Fred up the basement stairs to the kitchen. As he sat at the table, she puttered around, looking for items to make tea. It was almost like being at home, as if they'd woken normally.

"I have such a headache," Fred said.

"Yes dear, you've had a most traumatic night," Mrs Willis said, and to soothe her husband's nerves, she turned on the radio loudly to drown out the sound of flesh ripping and the lanky man's final screams.

Leg Me Call You *Sweetheart*

Waking up dead was a shock, considering I'd been alive a few days before. I struggled to remember. I'd been working in the shop, getting a leg of lamb out of the freezer for Mrs. Gardner. Out of the corner of my eye, movement, and then the side of beef falling. Damn that Jimmy Beck, he never hung the meat right!

In the darkness, I couldn't see. The only sound was the occasional settling of the dirt above. Normally I would have panicked; I'd been claustrophobic since my cousin Benny locked me in a closet when I was six. But this was comforting. The sound reminded me of childhood, playing trucks with Vinnie in his backyard. Even the smell was homey, a rich, clean smell of earth. I was just getting used to the idea of being dead when a shout startled me.

"Goddamn kids, I hate 'em!"

I sat up, not realizing I could until I did it. My head passed through the lid of the coffin and I found myself swimming up toward the surface. As my hand broke through the ground, I felt a cool breeze. I pulled myself out.

The cemetery was packed, people clustered beside the gravestones or walked among the trees. I watched in surprise. Something was odd about them. They looked translucent, I could almost see objects through their bodies, a bush or a headstone. Looking at my hands I noticed the same thing about me. We were ghosts.

"Little monsters."

At the edge of a small pond, a tall, scowling man picked shards of broken beer bottles out of his grey suit. Beside me an old guy sat against a tombstone and chuckled.

"Poor McGilly always has to put up with people tossing things on him." The old man shook his head. "That's what ya get for messing with the mob."

"What happened to him?" I asked.

He gestured at the pond. "Buried in concrete. Nobody alive knows he's there." He cocked his head. Blurred print from the tombstone's inscription showed through his face as he studied me. "Hey, you're new here. Dominic Gianno, says your stone."

"Yes, I just woke up."

The old guy clapped his hands. "Well, terrific. A neighbor. Hey folks, we got a new one!"

Shuffling over to greet me, the ghosts dressed like a history of fashion. Older ghosts wore faded suits, their faces almost totally transparent, their movements slow and devoid of feeling. The more recent dead were more solid. Jacob, explained how the oldest of the ghosts faded altogether. No one could see them. Some speculated they passed onto another state or were reincarnated. But no one worried. Death was a great stress reliever.

"We only come out at night," Vic from the pond said. He brushed the final specks of glass from his brown hair. "Sunlight makes us fade faster. You're only supposed to fade naturally, ya know."

I pointed at the pieces of glass scattered on the ground around him. "How does that stuff stick to you. You're a ghost."

Vic grinned, one end of his mouth curving in a crooked fashion around his scarred cheek. "After a couple hundred years you can't move anything but recent ghosts can still touch and feel physical stuff. It's great fun on Halloween. I'll get revenge on those little buggers." He grabbed my arm, his beefy fingers digging into my ghost flesh.

He laughed as I tried to pull away.

"How can you do that?"

"I've only been dead for five years, you've been dead a few days. We're still pretty young," Vic said, "as far as being dead goes. We're solid to each other. Won't start to fade for a while."

"So these people can touch each other?" I gestured at the other ghosts standing beneath the trees.

"Yeah, don't usually though." Vic shrugged and released my arm. "They lose interest in those sorts of thing."

He pulled out a pack of waterlogged cards and shuffled. "Wanta play some poker?"

By the time I returned to my coffin, I owed Vic three million dollars. Good thing we weren't alive or I'd be in big trouble. Vic cheated but I couldn't figure out how. Not that it mattered; I had eternity to win back my honour.

In my coffin, my body looked the same as before death; black hair, bushy eyebrows, large nose and thin lips. The dark blue suit was the one I'd worn to my sister's wedding three years ago with the stain on the left arm where my uncle had spilled his wine while trying to pick up my date. I had never gotten around to getting a new suit and certainly my mother hadn't bothered. Now it would never matter. I dismissed the thought as I felt the familiarity of my physical hands, arms, torso, left leg, right leg.

Right leg again.

Three legs?

I shot out of my coffin like a bat out of hell.

Sunlight burned my eyes. I gulped for air and then,

realizing how stupid that was, stopped. Stay calm. So something was in my coffin. So what? I was already dead, nothing worse could happen to me now.

Chiding myself for being silly, I returned to my coffin and cautiously began to explore. Surprisingly my physical body moved easily. The hand flopped over and back, passing through my ghost face as I felt around. I counted body parts until I found an extra one that didn't belong.

Smooth, soft skin. Definitely not mine, my skin was hairier than that, my mother's side of the family. I traced the outline with my hands.

A leg, severed above the knee. What the hell was an extra leg doing in my coffin?

That night I tried to pull it up to the surface but the leg stopped at the coffin lid. Not a ghost leg. I left it behind.

Vic sat beside the pond, shuffling cards in his oversized hands. A smile lit up his ugly face. "Ready for another game?"

I shook my head. Jacob also sat beside the pond. He chuckled.

"He's caught onto you, Vic, you're going to have to find another sucker."

Vic swore enthusiastically. I guess God never really cared about cursing.

I interrupted Vic's soliloquy. "There's a leg in my coffin and it's not mine."

"Then whose is it?" Jacob asked, amused.

"That's what I'd like to know."

Vic leaned back against a large rock, his skin turning the rock's shade of grey. "Hey, Dom, where'd ya say you were from before you died?"

"Crawford."

"No, I mean the funeral parlor. Where did they take you when the beef fought back?"

I threw up my hands. "How should I know? I was dead."

"Come on, don't be an idiot," Vic said. "Think about it."

My family wasn't rich so my service would have been small. They hadn't spent much on the coffin. Fake silk and smelly fiberglass.

"Belmont's Funeral Parlor, probably. My father couldn't afford much better."

"Ah, now that explains it." Vic smiled with satisfaction.

"Huh?"

"Your leg. The funeral director at the Belmont, he takes left-over limbs and buries them for a price. Pretty sweet deal."

I couldn't believe what I was hearing. "You mean somebody is buried without their leg?" I said. "Would their ghost be missing a leg too?"

"Don't be a putz," Vic said. "The leg is from somebody living. Someone sending a message to the owner. Next time they won't be losing just a leg, is my guess."

I couldn't concentrate on cards. Vic wandered away, shaking his head in disgust. An abandoned leg seemed tragic to me. I wondered again about what would happen once the owner of that leg died. Would he or she be handicapped in death as in life, a one legged ghost, forced to wander the night?

"More likely hop the night," Jacob joked when I expressed the thought. I frowned as he laughed.

None of the others seemed bothered. I couldn't understand them. Moonlight shone through the clouds, lighting up the gentle hills. After spending my life in the city, the grass and the maples dotting the land were fascinating. The ghosts were another story.

Beside Vic and Jacob, the other ghosts didn't speak to me or each other. They just wandered around. I tried to tell them about the leg but they stared at me, as if I was some kind of alien.

My frustration grew. How could they not be affected, how could they just stare... lifelessly. I chuckled to myself. A stupid thing to think.

The sunrise did little to lift my depression. In my coffin, the leg lay on the polyester-cum-silk, toes pointing toward my body's crotch. Even though I was dead, the idea of it made me uncomfortable. Maneuvering the leg was a challenge; I keep falling out of the coffin into the surrounding dirt. Finally I managed to squeeze it down to the far end.

Settling into my body, I felt the decay already setting in.

I couldn't help wondering about the owner of the leg. What had she done to deserve having her leg amputated? Maybe Vic was wrong and she'd been involved in a horrible accident, maybe a car crash. Then why would her leg have been hidden in my coffin? Was she still in danger from whomever had done this to her?

That evening I floated up, determined to play cards with Vic and not think about the leg. I had to start acting like the other ghosts. Dispassionate, detached.

Staring at the faded faces of the cards I couldn't stop pondering the leg. How was the unknown owner coping?

"Are you still mooning over that bloody leg?" Vic said.

"What? No, I'm not." I shuffled my cards again. Still terrible.

"Come on, it's your turn."

As we finished the game, Vic winning of course, he leaned across the rock we used as a table. "Hey, since it's such a big deal, can I see it?"

My head jerked. Possessiveness clutched me. Why did he want to see it? I studied him through narrowed eyes. He'd made fun of it all night and suddenly, he was struck by the desire to see it.

Vic gazed at me, unaware of my churning emotions.

"Another time," I mumbled. I picked up the cards and shuffled.

But he just couldn't leave well enough alone. "Come on, let me see it."

I shook my head, not trusting my voice. I had a sudden image of Vic, his hands gently stroking the leg, my leg.

"Ah come on, Dom."

"No," I exploded, throwing the cards. They scattered around the nearest graves. "It's my leg and you can't have it!"

Ghosts turned at my outburst. Vic sat back, astonishment etched into his face. He spread his hands in a conciliatory gesture.

I turned and dove into the ground, away from their questioning looks. I'd had enough of their snarky remarks, their superior attitude. I spent the rest of the night in my coffin, stroking the smooth skin of the leg.

Sometime later I sensed another presence. I stiffened.

"Are you okay?" Jacob asked.

I swallowed, embarrassed. I'd made such a big fuss, but I couldn't explain how I felt. I tried to be detached, to not think about it, but all I could do was picture the owner, staring up a flight of stairs.

"I'm sorry, Jacob."

"That's okay, son." He paused for a moment. "Do you want to talk about it?"

"I don't know what there is to talk about," I said truthfully.

"How about how you're obsessed with that leg."

I blinked into the darkness. That was ridiculous. Ghosts couldn't obsess about anything.

I am not, I meant to say. Instead it came out, "You're right."

And he was right, I knew it the moment the words left my mouth. Of all the craziest things, here I was dead and obsessing over somebody's lost leg.

"I'm trying to be a good ghost," I said.

Jacob chuckled. "What's a good ghost, Dom? I know you're feeling disoriented and confused right now. That's normal, believe me. You're adjusting." His tone became serious. "But you have to find out who that leg belongs to."

"How can I do that?"

"Go to the Belmont, there's bound to be records of where the funeral director gets the parts." Jacob paused. "Vic would know best how to do it."

"Do you think he'd help," I asked sheepishly. "After the way I spoke to him?"

"Only one way to find out, son."

Vic managed to keep a straight face through my whole apology, and seemed to take my feelings in stride.

"Don't sweat it, Dom," he said. "I know what to do."

The next day, we went out. I hadn't been in the daylight since my death, excluding when I'd discovered the leg. Odd to see the cemetery during the day, to see real people walking down the narrow paths and not be able to see through them.

"Can't they see us?" I asked Vic.

"Nah, you've got to concentrate for them to see you and yell real loud if you want them to hear you."

The Belmont Funeral Parlor was a small, cheap building with worn looking banisters leading up to smudged doors. Just the sort of place my father would patron.

Vic seemed to know the layout so I followed his lead. We ended up in the funeral director's office.

After a brief search, we found his personal files. I was surprised the director kept such detailed records.

Vic grinned wolfishly. "The better to black-mail his clients. I know this clinic. They do under the table work. No questions asked. Maybe your girl didn't want to go to a hospital, didn't want any questions."

We struck off to the small nondescript clinic on the west side. The clinic was on the second floor at the end of a dingy hallway. We slipped through the wall and into a tiny file room.

"How's your night vision?" Vic asked.

"I can't read in the dark."

Vic flicked on the lights and shook his head. "You newly dead," he mumbled.

We started pouring over the files, Vic at the A's and me at the Z's. I'd finished one drawer when the door flew open.

Two burly guards rushed in, hands clenched around ugly looking black sticks. Dread froze me.

Vic grinned as the guards started searching the aisles. "Time for some fun," he said.

"Vic..."

Too late. Vic yanked the back of one of the guards' pants. The man howled, dropping his stick. Falling to his knees, he grabbed his crotch.

The other guard spun, sweeping the room with his stick extended. Vic picked up the fallen stick and twirled it above his head. Ominously, he moaned.

The guard's face drained of colour. He stumbled back.

"Vic, that's enough."

"Hey, no way, this is great!" Vic started toward the terrified guard, moaning louder.

"Hey, stop!" I grabbed for the stick and we began tugging it back and forth.

"Let go," I said. "We've got work to do."

"No, I'm having fun."

"Enough of your fun."

Both guards stared at the stick waving back and forth. We'd shouted loud enough for them to hear us. I let go; Vic flew back through the wall. The stick clattered to the ground.

With a yelp, the guards fled, slamming the door. Vic poked his head in and grinned.

"What were they doing here?" I asked.

"All these kinds of clinics hire muscle, to protect their on-premises stash. No prescriptions to write, no paper trail, more profit. But they have to make sure no kids get in to steal the stuff."

"Great," I said. "Let's get back to work."

Hours later we were still pouring over the files. I was getting thoroughly bored when Vic yelled.

"Found it!"

I scrambled over to him and we spread out the file.

"Look," he said. "Thirty-two year old woman admitted on May 20th with penetrating wound to right knee. Blah blah blah. Removal of leg from knee down on May 22nd. Says something about septic. She lives on Mason Road." He pointed to the file. The name read Latisha Bryant.

I slapped Vic on the back. "Thanks, Vic."

He grinned. "What are your dead friends for?"

That night I made my way to Latisha's address. I had to see her, had to see the body to whom my leg had belonged.

She lived in a small bungalow. Slipping through

the oak door, I found myself in a living room enveloped in red plush carpeting, reflected in stripped mirrors along the far wall. An overstuffed green couch, empty of occupants, sat beneath the mirrors. With her back to me, a woman sat in a wheelchair, her remaining leg propped up on a stool, cushioned by a pillow. With a flick of her hand, she brushed back rich, red hair.

"I don't care what he says," she snapped into the phone. "He owes me and I'll get it from him." She paused, fingering the flowered robe she wore. "Look, if he doesn't pay me, I'm going to the cops. I don't care if he's the best john there is." She slammed down the phone.

Her deep, rich voice mesmerized me but one of the phrases nagged at me. John?

The door bell rang and Latisha called, "Come in."

A tall, black woman wearing a short, lime green coat and an even shorter skirt breezed through me, into the living room.

"Maureen, good to see you," Latisha said.

"Hi, honey. I picked up your prescription from the drug store. All the girls at the corner send their love. How are you doing?"

Latisha dumped the pill bottles onto the table beside her. "I don't know," she sighed. "I don't like this chair."

"Don't worry, you'll get used to it," Maureen said.

"I know. I just miss dancing."

"You knew better than to tangle with Leo."

Latisha's expression hardened. She squared her shoulders. "I couldn't let him hurt Martin. I was gonna stay working for him while we set up the bar. Now no way."

Maureen shuffled nervously. "Do you think that's a good idea? He'll be real upset."

Latisha's knuckles whitened on the armrests. "I don't care how upset Leo gets. I've finally got the chance to do something I want. I won't let that scum stop me, and I won't let him intimidate my partner." She reached over to take Maureen's hand. "You know, we could use a good waitress."

The black girl bit her lip.

"Don't answer. Just think about it." Latisha patted Maureen's arm reassuringly. "Think about having a real job. About Danny not being afraid to tell the other kids what you do for a living."

Tears formed in Maureen's eyes. "Leo," she whispered.

"You let me worry about Leo. That cheap bugger couldn't stop me before and I'll be damned if I let him now. He took my leg, but he can't take my dream. Next time he'll get more than he bargained for."

I left. Latisha was certainly a different image from the damsel I'd imagined. Despite her vulgar surroundings, her determination impressed me. Losing her leg had galvanized her spirit, made her aware of the preciousness of life.

Over the next week, I visited Latisha often. I learned her schedule of rising at eleven. She didn't returned to the streets but spent afternoons in an old rundown club on Dixie Boulevard. With no wheelchair access, she would knock on the wall until Martin, her short, balding business partner, came out and lifted her up the few stairs. Inside, the decor was late sixties, looking more the colour of vomit than psychedelic. Brown carpeting, worn right down to the wooden floor at spots, stopped halfway to the decrepit bar devoid of stools.

For days, I watched them plan and prepare.

Both had several friends looking for work. Latisha's aunt owned a used furniture business. Martin's cousin ran a paint factory.

But they weren't without problems. Leo's presence haunted them, more than I did. I had yet to see this man who had disabled Latisha and upset Martin. The little man would quiver, pushing his glasses up with face with pudgy fingers, stuttering nervously. Latisha would throw her hair back, eyes flashing in the dim light.

"I will not be extorted by a pig like Leo," she snarled.

"Latisha, tt..try to be reasonable." Martin placed a hand on her arm to placate her. "We're new at this. We can't afford tt..trouble right from the start. How long have I known you? Years. I know how you hate to be pushed around, but I don't think we have any ch..choice."

Latisha jabbed a finger in Martin's face. "It's that kind of attitude that lets that scumbag get away with what he does. If we stand up to him, others will too. Can't you see that, Martin?"

He shook his head. A now familiar shouting match ensued with Latisha leaving in a huff. I had to run to keep up as she sped down the street. Anger erased her clumsiness with the chair.

"Son of a bitch," she hissed to herself. "Won't intimidate me, I'm sick of cowering. Gotta show everybody what kind of idiot he really is." She steered onto her walkway, heading for the backyard.

When I returned to the cemetery that evening, Vic was waiting. He kept switching his cards from one pocket to another, a sure sign he had reached the limit of his patience.

"Come on, Dom, let me see her."

"Not now, Vic. I've got a lot to think about."

"Troubles in paradise? Maybe I can help."

Bark showed through Vic's face. His strong chin jutted out from beneath a low lying branch. He was more at home with the criminal element, he would know how to handle Leo.

"Okay," I said. "Maybe you can help."

At Latisha's house, I noticed the living room light on. It was still early so Latisha would be up, watching TV, making arrangements for the club. We slipped through the door into the living room. Nothing.

"So where is she?" Vic asked.

Ignoring him, I searched the house. No one home. Fear churned in my stomach.

Vic saw the look on my face against an abstract painting in the bathroom. "What's the matter?"

"She should be here," I mumbled. Maybe the club. It wasn't open yet, she could have gone to take care of something.

"Let's try out her bar," I told Vic.

The mottled steel door of the club posed no problem as we slipped through. Inside the main room was empty, the stage area still spotlit from the singing auditions earlier that day. Vic blanched at the sight of the place.

"They want to make this a night club?"

"It's taking a while," I said shortly. The empty room made me nervous. Where was Latisha?

A scream broke the silence.

Vic and I rushed to the back room. As I passed through the door, I saw Martin slumped against the wall. A trickle of blood ran down his cheek but he was still breathing.

Beside the back door, Latisha's wheelchair lay on its side, one wheel spinning slowly. The door opened to a narrow alley. Light spilled out on the cracked, greying concrete. I rushed outside.

Latisha lay in a heap, beside three bags of garbage. Her remaining leg sprawled out, her arms flung up over her head. Her red hair spilled across the alley floor like a blanket of blood. Vic came up behind me.

I turned her over. Blood soaked her dress from stab wounds in her stomach.

"She's dying," I wailed.

"Stop her," Vic said.

"What, how?"

"Talk to her, make her fight. I'll call the ambulance and the police."

I grabbed his arm. "How?"

"She'll be closer to us, you'll be able to reach her. Convince her to hold on until the ambulance gets here."

Before I could protest he pushed me towards her. I felt myself falling through Latisha, through the concrete, inwards. Inwards. And down.

Pain drowned me. I thrashed my arms, trying to get oriented. A cry passed through me, echoing in my mind. Images crystallized. A big man, monstrously huge, loud voice shouting at a cowering woman. Momma. The word flashed in my mind, childish rage made the image shiver. I realized: this was Latisha.

"Latisha!" I called out.

Words, thoughts bubbled up around me. Who, where?

"I'm Dom," I said and stopped. What could I say now, that I'm dead and I have her amputated leg in my coffin? That I'd been haunting her, watching her work on the club?

Pain began seeping in. I had to get her to fight, to hold on until help arrived.

"Latisha," I said. "I've been watching you. You've got to hold on and fight. You're right, Leo can't win if you stand up to him. Others will help you but you've got to hang on."

Who ARE you? Curiosity pushed past the pain.

"I'm someone who loves you," I said and knew it was true. It didn't matter if once she'd worked the streets. She had more courage and spunk than anyone I'd ever known.

"I've got your leg," I continued. "It was buried in my coffin when I died. I'm taking care of it for you,

Latisha. For when your time comes, but that isn't now."

What the...? I could feel her confusion and disbelief. I knew exactly how she felt. I'd been feeling the same disorientation ever since I'd died. But she had risen to her challenge while I had floundered.

"You've got to hang on, Latisha. You've fought so hard, I know you'll be a success. Leo can't stop you, he'll never win if you don't let him."

Leo's name stirred up a swirl of anger. I cheered for her. As long as she wasn't succumbing to the pain, she could survive.

I became aware of Vic hovering close by. I separated from Latisha. Her breathing seemed stable. I felt hope.

"I called the ambulance. They'll be here any minute," Vic said. "But I think we've got other business."

He gestured down the alley. A large man, wearing jeans and a grey leather jacket, appeared dragging a brown drum. As we watched, he dumped the drum over. Vic grabbed my arm.

"Gasoline," he said. The clear liquid began spreading along the alley.

"He's going to torch the building," I said. This had to be Leo. He smiled when he saw Latisha's sprawled form and lumbered closer. Acne scars potted his face where an unsuccessful beard tried to cover them up. He had mean, little eyes.

"Give him the full treatment, Dom." Vic waved encouragement.

"Why don't you?"

"You're the one who's been dead the shortest time. It'll be easier for you."

The full treatment. I knew what that meant. I concentrated. First my feet, then my legs, then my torso. I pictured my entire body whole. Funny how something so simple was so difficult. I'd seen myself a million times in the mirror but had never really paid attention. Now I had to do it perfectly.

Slowly, I felt myself become solid. My short legs, thin arms, my black hair with its tendency to curl. Suddenly I appeared in front of Leo.

His little eyes widened. He took a step back.

"Get away from here." I tried to sound menacing and raised my arms. "If you come back I'll put a curse on you."

"Who the fuck are you?" Leo said.

"I am the ghost that haunts this bar. If you return I'll kill you."

"Forget that." Leo pulled back and swung.

His right fist sailed straight through my head. I smiled rather nastily and shouted, "BOO!"

His footsteps echoed off the stone walls as he ran.

Vic laughed, clutching his stomach. He stumbled and slipped through the garbage bags.

I looked down at Latisha. Her eyes were open. Could she see me? As I faded back into nothing, she lifted her hand. "Dom..."

The other ghosts were envious when I started receiving flowers at my grave every Sunday. On special occasions, we visited Latisha and Martin's new night club, appropriately titled "The Haunt". Vic took a liking to one of the waitresses, a short blonde with bad teeth. Leo never showed up again. For some reason, the name of the club deterred him.

Mostly, I hang around the cemetery talking to the older ghosts. I'm more relaxed now. Being dead isn't so confusing. I have plenty of time to mull things over.

Once in a while, I visit Latisha at her home. Maybe it's wishful thinking, but I believe she knows when I'm there. She'll look into the air with a wink and a smile, and she'll pat her stump.

I'm still taking care of her leg and one day, I know, we'll go dancing.

Living With the Dead

"Stop whining, Margie, and get your grandma," Momma said.

"But mom, she smells," Margie said, with a stomp of her foot.

"Just you hush about that now," Momma said. "She don't need to hear that kind of talk." Momma cast a furtive glance around, just in case anyone heard. "Now go get grandma."

Momma's insistent whisper finally nudged Margie into action. With a heavy sigh, Margie turned and headed back up the darkened path to the house. Why they were packing up the van in the middle of the night, she didn't know. First Dadda had gone off with the soldiers, then Uncle Paul, then the schools were closed due to contamination, and now they were packing up the van. She just knew Momma wanted to go on a road trip somewhere which was all fine if it was just her and Margie and Donny but grandma was all smelly now. Why did they have to bring her along?

She climbed the stairs of the porch, avoiding the third step which creaked. Momma was insisting they be quiet so as not to bother the neighbors. If they waited to pack the van tomorrow, that would solve that problem, Margie thought but no one ever asked her.

She eased open the door and slipped inside. The interior of the house was cooler than the heavy heat of the summer outside. In the pale light from outside, Margie saw the outlines of the furniture, each arm of the chairs and couch covered with crocheted doilies. The tables had crocheted centre pieces. Even the mantle had a crocheted cover. Grandma had gone a little nuts with the crocheting since grandpa died.

Margie slipped up the stairs. As she reached the top, she heard the telltale click of nails tapping on a hook. Grandma was crocheting again. Well, at least when she was doing that, she wasn't flapping her mouth and moaning at you, Margie thought.

The door creaked as she opened it but grandma didn't pause in her crocheting. A bomb could go off in here and grandma wouldn't drop a stitch. She sat in her rocking chair in the corner. Margie thought she would want to be near the window but Momma wouldn't let the chair sit there anymore. The neighbors might see. Margie didn't know why Momma worried so much about the neighbors. Would they want some of grandma's doilies?

To Margie's surprise, grandma was crocheting in the dark. Strange, she thought, but the old woman had been doing it for so long she could probably produce a pattern in her sleep. Margie crept across the floor and tugged on grandma's sleeve.

"Time to go, grandma," she said.

The old woman stopped rocking. "Uhh?"

She hardly ever talked in words any more. Just grunted. So annoying, thought Margie. She tugged harder on grandma's arm.

"Come on, we're going for a ride," she said. Then inspiration struck her. "You can bring your crocheting."

That elicited a grunt of excitement. Grandma rocked back and used the forward momentum to push her up onto her feet. She grabbed the bag of yarn at her feet. Margie hurried to fetch her favourite cardigan sweater. She draped it over grandma's shoulders. The old woman shuffled forward, but instead of heading for the door, she headed for the closet.

"Grandma, we have to go," Margie said.

Grandma waved at her and commenced fussing about in the bottom of the closet. With a heavy sigh, Margie headed over to see what was the matter. Grandma was picking up different balls of yarn and tossing them in the bag. Others, she threw farther into the closet. She'd spend all night sorting if I let her, Margie thought.

"That's enough, grandma, we have to go." Margie tugged on the old woman's sleeve but grandma ignored her. Okay, that was it.

Margie snatched the bag from grandma's hand and darted toward the door.

"Ahhhh!" Grandma turned to glare at Margie at the door.

"We have to go, grandma," Margie said. "Come on!"

The old woman's mouth closed in a pout. She clenched her bony fists so tight Margie thought her knuckles would pop through the skin.

"Come on, grandma," Margie said. "You can show me how to crochet on the trip. Would you please?"

Any question about crocheting caught grandma's interest. Her fists loosened and the pout faded from her face. She made a high pitched sound of excitement and started shuffling toward Margie.

Margie backed out of the room, coaxing grandma toward the stairs with a wave of the bag.

"Just think of all the new doilies we can make," Margie said.

Grandma followed her all the way to the van.

"I'm hungry, momma," Donny said several hours into the trip.

"Margie, give him a cracker, would you?" Momma kept both hands on the wheel and stared out the windshield. In the weak lights from the front of the van, Margie could see light standards lining the highway, disappearing into the darkness, but none of them were lit.

"Can I have one too?" Margie said.

"Just one for each of you."

Margie unwrapped the box of crackers and slipped her brother three and then took three for herself. She held a finger up to her mouth. Donny nodded. He might be a boy and younger than her but at least he knew when to shut up.

In the front passenger's seat, grandma hummed to herself, still crocheting away. Once in a while Margie noticed Momma glancing over at grandma before she turned to look at the road.

Through the rearview mirror, she thought she saw tears in Momma's eyes.

That was her first inkling that maybe this wasn't a normal trip after all.

"Momma." Margie kept her voice casual. "When will Dadda be home from the soldiers?"

Momma's hands tightened on the steering wheel. Beside Margie, Donny paused with a cracker halfway to his mouth. He stared over at his sister, as if in shock that she'd asked such a question.

Margie saw Momma's gaze flick up in the rear view mirror before she looked back at the road. "Just be quiet, Margie."

"But Momma..."

"I said be quiet!"

Even grandma's crochet needle stilled for a moment after Momma's outburst. When the silence lengthened, grandma's nails clicked on the needle and she started working again.

Margie sat back and watched Donny nibble on his cracker. His eyes looked big over top and shimmered with tears.

So he understood too.

They wouldn't be going home after this trip.

The tire blew out about an hour later. The van skidded down the asphalt. Momma twisted the steering wheel and hung on. Donny flew against Margie and before he could be knocked back, she wrapped her arm around him and hugged him close beside her. The squeal of the tires shrieked in Margie's ears, making her shoulders hunch up her neck. The darkness around them seemed to swirl then the van stopped moving, shuddering to a stop.

Momma sagged in the front seat. Even grandma sat still. Donny sniffed beside Margie but instead of pushing away from her like usual, he clung on.

Momma brushed several strands of brown hair from her face and twisted in her seat. "Everybody okay back there?"

"We're okay, Momma," Margie said. She felt Donny tremble against her. She tightened her arms.

"Okay," Momma said. "Everyone just stay in the van."

She undid her seat belt and then got out of the van. Margie saw her walk around the front. The yellow light gave her brown skirt a muddy look. She put a hand on her head the way she always did when facing a big problem. Her head tilted then shook slowly from side to side. After a moment, she turned her back to them and Margie thought she saw Momma's shoulders tremble in the headlights, but she couldn't be sure. Then Momma turned back around and she had a big smile on her face.

She came back and leaned in the driver's side window. "Change of plans everyone. We're going to campout tonight."

At the mention of campout, Donny pushed away from Margie. "Can we really, Momma?"

She nodded. "Yes, we can."

Donny gave a cheer but Margie wasn't so sure it was a great idea.

They gathered sleeping bags, some of the food and cookery from the back of the van. Grandma insisted on bringing along a bag of yarn and rather than argue with her, Momma let her bring it. They trudged a ways from the road, far enough to not be seen but to still have a glimpse of the van.

Momma spread out the sleeping bags, making sure the kids were in between Momma and grandma.

"Are we gonna have a fire?" Donny said.

"Not right now," Momma said. "In the morning we'll use one to cook breakfast."

"But what about now?"

"We don't need one now. You've already had your supper."

"But..."

"Hush now, Donny. Get in your sleeping bag and go to sleep."

Momma gave Donny that no nonsense tone. He stuck out his lip in a pout but climbed in the bag. Margie climbed into her bag but noticed that both Momma and grandma stayed out of theirs. Grandma was still crocheting and would until the end of time but Momma sat with her arms wrapped around her knees, looking out around them.

"Momma?" Margie said.

"Go to sleep, baby," Momma said. She kept looking around.

Margie stayed silent but she didn't sleep for a long time.

A snarling howl woke her up. She didn't really pay attention until she heard Momma cry out and Donny's scream. Then her eyes snapped open.

Early dawn light spilled across the sky. A whole group of people were surrounding them. Hunched, lumbering figures moaning and drawing closer. Momma clutched Donny to her. Grandma clutched her crocheting. Margie stood up from her sleeping bag, surveying the approaching figures.

They looked like nightmare people, faces slack, some covered in blood, others with sores or cuts that didn't heal. They lurched and reached with grabby hands. In a few minutes they would reach them and tear them apart. One of the figures even had a soldier's uniform on. Could that be one of the soldiers that took Dadda?

She felt panic clutch at her but she pushed it down. Screaming and crying like a baby wouldn't help and they were in real trouble. She had to think.

Momma was too busy with Donny and grandma was too busy crocheting. It had to be Margie.

She caught sight of grandma's crochet needle. Wait a minute. Grandma sounded just like these people. She had the same slack jawed look, the same moans. What if...?

Margie darted to grandma's side. She grabbed the bag of yarn and tossed the balls into the air. They fell into the crowd around them. Grandma howled. She grabbed at the empty bag in Margie's hands.

"Show them, grandma, show them what to do with the yarn," Margie said.

Grandma moaned and shook the empty bag.

"You still have your crocheting," Margie said. "Show them how."

She picked up grandma's discarded doily, half finished. She held it up above her head.

The moans around her changed in pitch. Now they sounded curious.

Grandma snatched the doily away from Margie. She stuck her crochet needle into it and started crocheting. The closest of the figures bent over to watch. One of them had a ball of yarn. He started plucking at it, trying to make his fingers work the same as grandma's.

Margie picked up one of grandma's extra croquet needles and held it out to the man. He took it from her, holding it the wrong way. Grandma snarled. She jumped forward, grabbed it from his hands, flipped it around and stuck it back between his fingers. Then she moaned and shoved her work forward, showing him how to move the needle.

After a few minutes, the man started crocheting. Within twenty minutes, all of grandma's five extra needles were being put to use. Margie organized the ones not crocheting into lines that wrapped and rewrapped the yarn.

Soon they all hummed and looked happy as they made doilies and table coverings.

Momma was the one who discovered they weren't only good at crocheting. Several liked painting and were patient even with intricate trim. She had them practice on an old barn out in a field. Soon the barn still looked sagging but the fresh coat of yellow paint made it look like a new sagging barn.

It took time for Momma to convince the town that there were better ways to deal with lurching, moaning people than fighting them. Some still tried to be bitie but if given fresh raw meat and some work to do, most were happy to crochet or paint or do whatever craft they were good at.

Soon they were able to return home and Momma was the first to have the whole house painted by them.

Before long, the rest of the neighborhood clambered for their chance.

For Margie, the best part was seeing all the lumbering, lurching forms carrying paint cans, or carving tools, or even the ones who sat on the porch with grandma and crocheted up a storm. They all hummed and tried to smile at her. Often the smiles looked like grimaces but she knew they were trying.

She could see it in their eyes. Especially the ones who tried to keep giving her doilies.

But the very best day was the day Dadda

returned from the soldiers. His eyes grew wide at the sight of all the crotcheters on the porch. He didn't even seem to notice when Momma came out to give him a hug or when Donny wrapped himself around Dadda's legs.

"What is going on?" he said.

"It's okay, Dadda," Margie said. "We figured it out. They just wanna help out."

"That's right, hon," Momma said. "You should see what they can do."

Dadda scratched his head. "I never wouldn't thought." He noticed the van in the driveway, still listing to one side where the tow truck had dumped it. It had turned out to not only be a blown tire but some other problem that Margie didn't understand.

"What happened to the van?" Dadda said.

"Momma broked it," Donny said. He laughed as Momma's cheeks turned red.

"Hmm." Dadda rolled up his sleeves. "Well, let's see if any of them are good with cars."

He ruffled Margie's hair before he headed over to the van. Before long, a few of the lurching folks staggered over to bend over the motor with Dadda. And just like Dadda thought, some of them were good with cars.

And with a whole lot of other things too. And over time, Margie found that even though they were still kinda smelly, she didn't mind it that much after all.

Puppy Love

andy Williams always thought of herself as a cat person until one Thursday afternoon, while killing some time waiting for her friend, Anita, to meet her drinks, she wandered past the River's Way Pet Store. She glanced in the front window where a group of puppies tumbled all over each other in play. She smiled at them then noticed one sitting in the corner, away from the others. A gray and black pup with pointed ears sat with his tail curled around his feet, blue eyes studying the puppies in front of him. Mandy stopped and watched him. One of the puppies extracted itself from the group and bounded over to the gray and black pup. It yapped in his face, teeth coming dangerously close to snapping on his snout. With one paw, the gray and black pup pushed the other puppy down and away, with a gentleness that surprised Mandy.

Then those blue eyes turned to look at her.

She found herself inside the shop standing at the front counter, saying that awful clichéd phrase: "How much is that puppy in the window?"

The animal attendant (as they called themselves) checked his list and announced he was three thousand dollars since he was a Husky mix.

"Mixed with what?" she said.

"I'm not sure, it doesn't say," the attendant said, who looked like he was barely out of high school. "We just got this batch in. They're very popular. We've already sold three of them."

"Three thousand dollars," she said. "For a mixed dog. Are you sure that's the right price?"

The attendant checked his list again, popping his gum. "Yep, that's it, lady."

She retreated from the store, taking a last, lingering look at the puppy as she walked past the window. His gaze locked on her and followed her as she passed out of sight.

"Mandy, there you are!" Anita appeared from around the corner. She embraced Mandy. "So great to see you, let's get that drink!"

She laced her arm through Mandy's and led her off. Mandy glanced back, hoping to see the puppy one last time but the window was soon lost from view.

She expected to forget about the puppy but found herself still thinking of him the next day at work. The blue order sheets crossing her desk reminded her of his soulful eyes looking at her through the window. She could almost feel him calling to her, asking her to rescue him from this horrid place.

But three thousand dollars…

Ridiculous, she couldn't believe she was contemplating getting a dog. She put it out of her mind and turned back to work. These orders weren't going to process themselves.

That evening she found herself reviewing her apartment, seeing how sections could be blocked off if she had a puppy. She went so far as to sketch it out on paper before she realized what she was doing.

"Oh this is silly," she said to the empty apartment. The paper ended up in the waste basket.

Saturday she went shopping downtown, wandering through shops, trying on blouses and pants for work. She needed a few new blouses but none appealed to her. Usually she loved shopping, the thrill of the hunt, but today it irritated her. After a quick lunch she was going to head home when she found herself on the same street as the pet shop. On a whim she wandered by again, just to take a look.

She wasn't actually shopping for a pet, it was just fun to look in the window.

She had to keep repeating that to herself.

Sure enough, several puppies lay in the front window display. She'd caught them at nap time, she thought. The puppies were curled around each other or lying on top of each other. So cute! She tried to see the black and gray one. Probably he was underneath. He seemed like he'd end up there.

After several moments of looking through the

window, trying to see all angles, she realized he was gone.

Someone had bought her puppy!

Her breath sucked in as if she'd been punched in the stomach. She grabbed the edge of the window frame to steady herself. Maybe she was wrong, maybe the puppy was still in the display, just hidden from view. More searching yielded nothing. She had to admit he was gone.

She stumbled away from the pet store. Tears blurred her vision. Why hadn't she said yes? Why hadn't she bought the puppy when she had the chance? Three thousand dollars, the logical part of her mind tried to interject but her sorrow overrode any logical concerns. Her puppy was gone. Now what was she going to do?

She returned home in a fog, not even realizing she was there until she walked into the empty apartment. No patter of little feet coming to greet her, no joyous bark of welcome, no wagging tail of happiness at her arrival. The apartment felt empty and stagnant. The décor she'd loved for years looked stale and lifeless. How could she live in such a place alone?

That night she begged out of her plans for dinner with friends and stayed home. Her dreams were filled with brooding, dark images that she couldn't remember upon waking. They just left her with a feeling of uneasiness and anxiety.

On Sunday, the pet store didn't open until noon. She spent the morning waiting, arriving downtown too early so she wandered the streets, checking her watch every five minutes to make sure she arrived right as the store opened. Finally by eleven fifty-five, she stood outside the shop as the attendant unlocked the door. She grabbed the handle even before he could open it for her.

"I'd like to ask about the puppies in the window," she said.

"Oh yes, they've been very popular," he said. "We only have a few left. Most of them have been spoken for or already taken."

"I know," she said. "I wanted some information about the black and gray one you had, a male, quiet. I stopped by yesterday but I didn't see him in the window." She took a deep breath. "Was he sold?"

"Let me check." With agonizing slowness, the attendant sauntered over to the front desk and tapped at the computer. Every tap seemed slower, his finger hesitating above the key before pressing it down. Mandy wanted to reach across the desk and slap him to make him move faster. Finally the attendant nodded at the screen.

"I remember that one. He started acting up and we had to segregate him. We're sending him back to the breeder."

Mandy's heart pounded. Not sold! He wasn't sold! "So he's still here then?"

"Yeah. We have him quarantined in the back."

"May I see him?"

The attendant frowned. "I don't know. We're sending him back because of behavioral problems. We don't usually let people see those dogs."

"Please," she said.

The attendant heaved a great sigh as if she was really putting him out. "Okay, but if my manager asks, this was your idea."

He locked up the cash register and led her down the length of the store. Unlocking the back door, he ushered her in after calling for the other attendant to watch the cash. Mandy stepped through into a cacophony of barks, meows, bird calls and all manner of sounds of scratching, digging, and shuffling. Not even trying to make himself heard over the racket, the attendant waved her on. Past a cage of meowing cats and around a stack of boxes, she came upon a large crate cage. The gray and black puppy stood howling at the top of its lungs.

"It's been doing that for days." The attendant crossed his arms. "See why we're sending him back? Who wants that?"

The noise around her faded until all she could hear was the melodic sound of the puppy howling. He tilted his head, shifting in his song, and saw her. His mouth shut. The howling stopped. The puppy stared at her with those blue eyes.

"Seems like a waste to send him back," she said, fighting to keep the eagerness from her voice. "All that work for nothing. How much to take him off your hands?"

"I don't know, it was commission. I don't know that we can lower the price," the attendant said. "Besides, he seems okay now."

"That's a shame." Mandy started to turn away. As if on cue, the dog started howling again.

The attendant frowned. "Let me check with my manager."

He left her standing by the crate. When she turned back, the puppy stopped howling. He sat down, his tongue lolling out, as if he was smiling at her. Mandy stepped closer to the crate.

"When they come back, keep howling. I need them to give you to me."

The dog's head bobbed as if he was nodding. At least it looked like a nod to Mandy. Her pounding heart steadied a little. Please let this work, she thought.

In front of her, the puppy stood up and started howling again. A moment later, the attendant arrived with his manager in tow. A girl that looked only a few years older than the attendant, the manager crossed her arms and pulled back her shoulders to try to give herself an air of authority.

"You were asking about this puppy," she said.

"That's right," Mandy said. "Seems a lot of trouble for you to send him back to the breeder. What can you do for me if I take him?"

The manager's frown matched the attendant, as if both had been trained to do it. "I'm not sure we can sell him because of the behavioral problems. We can't back that."

"I'd be willing to sign a waiver," Mandy said. "If we can come to terms."

The frown lessened and a crafty look overtook the girl's face. "You'd be willing to accept the risk and not come back on us?"

"If we can come up with a reasonable price," Mandy said.

"Why don't we go somewhere quiet to discuss it," the manager said.

Mandy kept him crated for the ride home. In her living room, she didn't even hesitate to unlock the door and open it wide. The puppy stepped out, looking all the world like he belonged. He walked up to her and licked her hand. She dropped to her knees and threw her arms around his neck.

His tail wagged in a blur. Heat from his body warmed her own. Under her hands, his fur felt silky smooth.

He fit perfectly into her life, never barking too much, playful but aware of his surrounding so never knocking over delicate objects. He never made a mess and always let her know when he needed to go outside.

She named him Max. He seemed like a Max to her, mature, aware and dignified.

She hated putting a collar and leash on him but the vet insisted she do it, to protect the puppy from being picked up as a stray. Even on the first visit to the vet, he was well behaved. When she took him into the examination room, she explained that the vet was going to give him his shots. Over his head, she saw the vet smile but she knew Max understood her. He almost nodded but caught himself.

He only whined once after the first needle.

Everyone commented on what a good dog he was, on how well she'd trained him. After trying to correct them, she stopped and just smiled. No one understood how she and Max communicated, how she knew just what he was thinking and how he seemed to know what she wanted. He knew when to curl up beside her and when to stay in the corner until she was ready for company.

It was three weeks of bliss.

One Tuesday morning, she noticed that Max seemed out of sorts. He stuck his nose in the food bowl when she freshened his kibble but didn't eat anything. He didn't drink any water. Although he went outside at her urging, he only nosed around the sidewalk, finally peeing after the third time she told him. Afterward, he slunk home behind her, tail almost dragging on the ground.

Back in her apartment, she checked on him. Felt his nose, looked in his eyes and ears, ran her hands over his body to check for any strange lumps; nothing. He seemed normal. Except that he stared in her eyes, whining and this time, she didn't know what it meant.

She wanted to stay home with him but it was month end and she had several reports due.

"I'm sorry," she told him as he followed her to the door. "I'll be home as soon as I can."

He whined again. His tongue gave a brief lick to her fingers. She cupped his muzzle and kissed his forehead.

The whine reverberated in her ears and in her heart all the way to work.

The day dragged and sped by at the same time. Mandy barely had time to breathe between meetings and briefings but every spare moment, her mind returned to Max, worrying about him, wondering if he was okay at home. The dog walker, instructed to call with any problem, didn't call. So there must be no problem but it didn't stop her from worrying.

Her final meeting stretched to almost seven o'clock. She skipped the subway and hailed a cab. Reaching home, she tossed bills at the driver, jumped out of the cab and then ran for her apartment.

For the first time when she opened the door, Max wasn't there to meet her.

She found him huddled on his dog bed by the mantle. His body quivered under her hands as she knelt down and pet him. The whine sounded weak and thready.

"Oh Max, what's wrong?" she said.

He couldn't tell her.

She debated taking him to the after hours animal clinic but when she mentioned it, he shied away from her, retreating to his crate in the corner. She only managed to coax him out with a promise not to take him.

As the evening wore on, she forgot about food and sat by his dog bed, petting him, talking to him, trying to sooth him. Shivering quaked his body. She felt the heat radiating off his skin through his fur. Tears stung her eyes. He was sick and she should have taken him to the animal clinic. Maybe there was still time. She stumbled to her feet just as Max gave out a first howl of pain.

His body uncoiled. His legs shot out from under him. He landed on his belly and lay writhing. Howls and whines filled her ears. His blue eyes expressed an agony she couldn't comprehend. She fell to her knees in front of him.

"Max!" she said.

The puppy tried to lick her hand but another shudder shook his body. The skin under his fur undulated. He stretched out a paw to her. A howl broke from his lips. She took hold of the paw. The skin felt loose in her palm. As he shook, his paw pulled away, leaving fur and skin clenched in her hand. She stared down at it, stared at the paw. No, not a paw. What?

The digits of his paw elongated. The nails shortened and flattened. As she watched, the palm area expanded. His body rippled, muscles shifting and changing under his skin. Fur fell out in clumps. Legs stretched. His torso and muzzle contracted. Mandy's mouth dropped open as Max's face flattened and broadened. Skin and fur sloughed off, leaving pink flesh and a new body behind.

A human body.

Max sagged back on the floor, panting as the final throngs of his change rippled through him. Mandy knelt, staring at the man lying on her floor. But when he looked at her with those blue eyes, she knew it was Max.

Her Max.

"Come on, you need a shower." She took his arm and helped him stand. He seemed uncertain on two legs. They wobbled as he tried to walk and she had to support him the entire way. In the bathroom, he collapsed in the shower. She turned the water to warm and left him there. She needed to clean up the living room.

The mess was already drying and flaking. She pulled out the vacuum and managed to vacuum the worst of it away. The rest she wiped up with paper towels and tossed out. By the time she was finished, Max had learned to stand on his two feet in the bathroom. His stance looked a bit off. He stood on the balls of his feet, letting his arms hang in front of him. He almost looked like he wanted to fall forward onto all fours.

She turned off the water and held open a towel for him. Dripping, he stepped into it. As she wrapped it around him, feeling the new human body, he leaned forward and licked her cheek. Her skin tingled with the feel of his tongue.

To distract herself from her own confusion, Mandy toweled his black hair dry. She stepped back and he moved to follow her, letting the towel covering his body fall to the floor. She grabbed it and wrapped it around him.

"Hold here." She moved his hand until he grasped the edges of the towel. His brows drew together as he concentrated on holding with his hand. As she let go and he held onto the towel, he smiled, letting out a yip of triumph.

"Stay." She hurried to her bedroom and dug out an old cloth robe that was too big for her. She returned to the bathroom and helped him into it. His body coordination improved even as she watched and he even figured out how to tie the belt.

In the living room, sitting on the couch took him a few moments to figure out. He kept looking at his legs and she could almost hear him trying to think it through. Finally he managed to lower himself onto the couch without falling. The smile blazing across his face made her heart pound with joy.

She sat down, still not really sure what to make of this or how she felt about it. Her beloved dog had turned into a man. How? She didn't know or understand it.

"Can you talk? Can you understand me?" she said.

He opened and closed his mouth, as if trying to imitate her. Various yips and sounds came from his throat as if he was trying out his larynx but hadn't gotten the hang of it yet. Okay, so talking not an option at the moment, she thought. He might figure it out, just like he figured out how to walk on two legs and sit down like a human. He probably needed more time.

"Are you hungry?" she said.

His posture straightened and he yipped aloud. He wiggled on the couch as if trying to wag a nonexistent tail.

She pursed her lips to stop the laughter. "I'll get you something to eat."

In the kitchen she paused. What kind of food? Well, he was a human now so human food, but something basic. She didn't want him to get sick. She settled on grilling a steak and a few small potatoes. Adding a glass of water, she carried the food out to the dining table. Max stood up as she set it down. He hurried over, his gate more sure. She pulled out the chair for him. He studied it a moment and then sat down.

"You might as well learn how to use utensils right away." She held up the knife and fork.

It took several tries before he managed to hold them properly and even longer before he could hold the steak in place and cut it. The food was cold by the time he figured it out but he didn't seem to notice. Every piece cut and chewed was a triumph. She sat beside him, laughing at his obvious delight. He hummed aloud at her pleasure.

She stayed up all night teaching him different aspects of being human. Grasping with his hands was the most challenging. As the night wore on, he tried resorting to biting but she stopped him, encouraging him to try again with his uncooperative hands. Finally, she realized he was getting tired and needed to rest.

"Come on, Max, it's time to get some sleep," she said around three thirty.

"Yep," he managed to say, the word coming out halfway between a yip and a word.

Now another consideration, his dog bed was too small for his body now. She didn't have a guest room and only the one queen-sized bed in her bedroom. How odd would it be to sleep with her now-human dog in her bed?

There wasn't any other choice. She led him into the bedroom. She gave him a pair of her bike shorts and instructions on how to put them on, then she took her night clothes into the bathroom. When she returned after washing her face and brushing her teeth, he had the shorts on, although backwards. He seemed so pleased, she couldn't bear to correct him.

They both collapsed onto the mattress. He curled against her back. She felt the side of his face against her shoulder blade and the gentle warmth of his breath caressed her skin. She blinked and was asleep.

She woke up at seven feeling refreshed even with the lack of sleep. She stretched, twisting her body to the left and looking over her shoulder, expecting to see Max. He was gone. She sat up.

"Max?"

A familiar noise came from the living room, then the sound of paws clipping on the floor.

Max walked in. On four legs.

In his dog form.

"Max, what happened?"

He barked and jumped up on the bed. He pressed his nose against her hand. She touched his fur and found it sticky.

What the hell was going on? She pushed herself out of bed and headed for the living room. Max padded after her. In the centre of the room, she found a drying mess of flaking skin. He'd changed from his human form back into the dog form.

She stared down at the dog sitting beside her. Had she imagined it? Maybe she was working too hard and only dreamed of her dog turning into a man. Max stared up at her face. He licked her hand and whined.

Crazy, it had to be or she had hallucinated. She had been working hard lately. Maybe she needed a vacation or a couple of days off. She'd ask when she got in today.

She vacuumed up the mess, dressed and was out into the world. All day her mind kept trying to return to the memory of her human Max, how comfortable and safe she felt with him. But it was ridiculous, he was only a dog and while she loved him, she loved him as a pet. That was all.

That evening, he still didn't meet her at the door.

Again she found him whining and shivering in his dog bed. The change came quicker and not as painful as the first time. This time he seemed to expect it. As he stumbled to the bathroom to wash the residue off, she sat on the floor, trying to make sense of what was going on. Only when the shower turned off did it occur to her to check the calendar.

It was a full moon.

No, that couldn't be it. It was impossible.

As impossible as the man stepping out the bathroom with the towel wrapped around his waist?

"Mmmmm Mandy." He grinned as he managed to pronounce her name. Even standing still, she could almost feel him vibrating, as if he ached to wag his tail.

She shook her head. It was too much to deal with.

"What's going on?"

The smile on his face faded at the sound of her distress. He hurried to kneel in front of her. He whined at the tears of confusion that traced down her cheeks. His tongue appeared between his lips but he reached out with a hand to touch her cheek.

"'thorry," he said, unable to pronounce the 's' properly.

She took his hand, felt the real fingers pressed in her palm. A full moon and her puppy changed into a man. A reverse lycanthropy? How was it possible? How could it be real?

She couldn't deny it was real, as real as Max kneeling in front of her, her distress reflected on his face. He whined in his throat, unable to express himself in words.

He needed her to help him learn to be human. She had to hold on to that.

She stood up and held out her hand to him. "Come on, Max. Time for more lessons."

He changed for a total of four nights a month. By the end of the fourth night, he'd learned to hop into the bathtub for the change, making clean up easier. Although she missed talking with him when he was in his dog form, she knew now for sure that he understood her.

They became even better companions.

One evening, two days before the next full moon and his change, she took him for his final evening walk a little later. She'd gone to see a play with Anita so instead of being able to walk Max at eleven, it was closer to midnight. The summer evening air felt warm and fresh on her skin. After the sticky humidity of the day, it was nice to walk about the street with a cool breeze.

Max also seemed to enjoy the walk. He bopped

along the sidewalk, stopping to sniff at various important spots, checking the neighborhood news as he'd explained to her in his human form.

They stopped in front of the old Miller place, a decaying house that spouted a to-be-demolished sign at least two years old. Some legal squabble between relatives and the city left the house in legal limbo. Another year or so and they wouldn't need to demolish it, Mandy thought. The place would fall down on its own.

Max stood with his nose stuck in the grass beside the road, his back to the house. Mandy faced the house. She didn't want to turn her back on it, just in case. The knee high grass could hide any manner of things and she wanted to stay alert.

The breeze ruffled the grass in front of the house. It carried the scent of sweet flowers from the garden two houses down. She listened to Max sniffling and scratching behind her. Such a perfect evening.

A snarl shattered the silence. A shadow leapt at her from the grass. Hot, sour breath filled her face as a muzzle snapped at her. She staggered back. A mutt with mangy fur growled at her. Max lunged past her, howling a challenge. He and the mutt clashed, mouths snapping, claws tearing. Mandy staggered, trying to hang on to Max's leash. The mutt was almost twice Max's size, it would injure him for sure. She had to stop the fight! Frantic, she looked around as the two dogs fought. There, a large stick. She grabbed it and swung at the mutt. It hit the side. The mutt didn't even seem to notice. She swung again, this time hitting the snout. The mutt whined and pulled away. She hit again and again, only connecting about half the time, but the rain of blows forced the mutt to back away. She yanked on Max's leash, dragging him back. Over excited, Max tried to lunge after the mutt. Mandy blocked his path, brandishing the stick at the mutt. Behind her, Max surged forward again, mouth snapping, claws reaching. The mutt leapt forward to respond. Mandy brought the stick down hard on its muzzle. The stick cracked. Part of flew back at her. She felt a scratch on her leg. The mutt squealed and jumped away. Shaking its head, it turned and ran back through the grass toward the decaying house.

Max tried to follow but Mandy yanked the leash again.

"Stop it, Max, stop!"

Finally he listened and stood on the sidewalk, mouth open, his tongue lolling forward as he panted for breath. Mandy held on to the stick, just in case. Her heart pounded in her chest. Fear made her legs tremble. She felt something warm on her left calf. She glanced down and saw blood. Damn, she'd cut herself.

"Come on, Max, we're going home." She tugged on the leash and this time he followed.

She took a shower when she got home to wash the grime off herself. The cut on her leg stung and oozed blood in a slow pulse. After the shower, she bandaged it. Odd that such a shallow cut would keep bleeding but maybe it was deeper than it looked.

In the living room, Max sat in his dog bed, head hanging down. He looked almost embarrassed.

"It's all right," she said. "Just don't do it again."

His tail wagged. She patted his head and wished him a good night.

Her leg throbbed as she lay in bed, trying to sleep. A burning sensation started under her skin and flowed over her body. Her nerves tingled.

Her bones ached. She opened her mouth to cry out but her jaw thrust outward. Her face twisted, skin breaking as the muscles and bones pushed forward. Agony twisted her body. A scream caught in her throat. She tried to turn away from the pain, her body twisted and...

She fell on the floor. Bedsheets tangled around her legs. Her alarm clock beeped at her. Sunlight peeked around the bedroom curtains. She ran her hands over her body. Nothing. No burning, no pain. Her face was normal. Her body was her own.

A nightmare. That was all.

She sighed in relief and got up to get ready for the day.

That night she stood with Max in the bathtub, waiting for his change. She sat on the edge of the tub as he sat inside. It was so much easier to rinse out of the tub after his change and he could shower at the same time. Under the bandage, her leg itched. She fought the urge to scratch it. It might leave a scar if she did that. Her skin was sensitive and had a tendency to scar. She didn't want to make it any worse.

But the itch turned to burning. She dug her fingernails into her palms, holding her hands tight on her lap to stop from scratching. The burning flared up her leg to her thigh, the nerves throbbing. Her shoulders hunched. As she moved them, she felt her muscles shift and keep shifting even when she stopped moving them.

In the tub, Max whined. His nose touched her left arm. He licked her.

She tried to turn toward him, tried to speak, but her mouth couldn't open properly. Her body twisted, teetered on the edge of the tub, and then she fell onto the floor. Pain shot through her. She tried to scream but only a gurgle came out. Her vision blurred with tears of agony. Her bones ached, her muscles tore. She felt her nerves searing inside her. She was dying!

Finally her mouth could open. She tried to talk. A howl filled her ears. Max calling her!

Then she felt hands touching her body. Someone lifted her up and placed her in the tub. She tried to stand on her legs, but they trembled too much and she fell forward, putting her arms out to catch herself. She landed on her front...

Paws.

Mandy whined as she saw the dog paws in front of her. She tried turn her head, look at the rest of her. Every part she could see was dog. The whine grew louder.

Max, his human form still wet from his own change, sat on the edge of the tub.

"I'm sorry," he said. "I didn't realize I scratched you." He reached out and patted her head.

"Don't worry, Mandy, I'll take care of you."

Mandy looked into his deep blue eyes and saw the understanding in them. He would look after her just as she looked after him. They both understood each other. Now they were the perfect companions.

She turned her head and licked his hand.

ABOUT THE AUTHOR

REBECCA M. SENESE weaves words of horror, mystery, contemporary fantasy, and science fiction in Toronto, Canada. She is the author of the contemporary fantasy series, the Noel Kringle Chronicles featuring the son of Santa Claus working as a private detective in Toronto. She garnered an Honorable Mention in "The Year's Best Science Fiction" and has been nominated for numerous Aurora Awards. Her work has appeared in numerous Holiday Hijinks anthologies including *Whimsical Winter Wonderland*, *Happy Holiday Historicals*, *Tidbits & Tinsel Tales*, *Haunted Holidays*, *Mistletoe Merriment*, *Crazy Christmas Capers*, and *Toy Trucks and Teddy Bears*. She has also appeared in *Home for the Howlidays*, *Pulphouse Fiction Magazine*, *Unmasked: Tales of Risk and Revelation*, the *Obsessions Anthology*, *Fiction River: Superpowers*, *Fiction River: Visions of the Apocalypse*, *Fiction River: Sparks*, *Fiction River: Recycled Pulp*, *Tesseracts 16: Parnassus Unbound*, *Tesseracts 15: A Case of Quite Curious Tales*, *Ride the Moon*, *Hungar Magazine*, *On Spec*, *TransVersions*, and *Storyteller*, amongst others.

FIND ME ONLINE

RebeccaSenese.com
RebeccaSeneseBooks.com